PESTIFEROUS QUESTIONS

A LIFE IN POEMS

PESTIFEROUS QUESTIONS

A LIFE IN POEMS

MARGARET ROZGA

ISBN: 978-1-943170-22-7

Cover Art & Cover Design: Wendy Vardaman
wendyvardaman.com

Interior Design: Jane L. Carman

Margaret Rozga photo: Josiah Werning

Jessie Benton Frémont at home in Los Angeles, California, 1902,
Online Archive of California, Photo: C. Wharton James

1846 Map of Texas, Oregon, and California: Samuel Augustus Mitchell

"On to Victory!," Courtesy, American Antiquarian Society

Published by Lit Fest Press, Carman, 688 Knox Road 900 North,
Gilson, Illinois 61436

Outside the box

*Editors have written to me for your biography & likeness, but I had no orders
from you & then you never told me how old you were yet.
How old are you?*

Jessie Benton Frémont to John Charles Frémont, June 1846

ON TO VICTORY!

TUNE SUSANNAH.

Our country's call we hear to day,
  We will be deaf no more,
We'll buckle on our armour,
  Its honor to restore.
Then let us all united be,
  So firm, and so true,
And all its foes we'll scatter so,
  They'll know not what to do.

CHORUS.—"Then on to Victory,"
    Our motto it shall be
      Then clear the way for Fre. and Day,
      And Kansas shall be free.

When Freemen dare to raise their voice,
  For Freedom in debate,
Some sneaking churl with percha cane,
  Will crack them o'er their pate ;
But they will find if that's the game,
  That more thar one can play,
A Senate Hall is not the place,
  The bludgeon to display.

CHORUS.—Then on &c.

The Buchaniers may loudly talk,
  Of what they mean to do,
But they will find they are too late
  To run their coaches through ;
For on the track we've put a nag,
  We're sure he is bound to win,
"One hundred miles a day" we think
  Can't fail to bring him in.

CHORUS.—Then on &c.

For Fremont now 'is the rallying cry,
  It comes on every breeze,
While Pierce and Douglass, you will find,
  Are shaking in their knees.
Old "Buck" he thinks the goal is won,
  And the White House all in view,
But we'll give them "Jessie" by-and-by
  For that we're pledged to do.

CHORUS.—Then on &c.

                              UNION.

ACKNOWLEDGMENTS

Grateful acknowledgment is made to the American Antiquarian Society for a Creative and Performing Artists and Writers Fellowship to do the necessary research and to the AAS staff and fellows who offered helpful suggestions and an encouraging environment at every step of the way.

Thanks also to the Rutherford B. Hayes Presidential Library and Museums in Fremont, Ohio for making their Frémont papers available to me.

I am grateful to editors of publications where versions of these poems originally appeared: *Philadelphia Review of Books Editor's Blog*, "At the Worcester Museum of Art" and *Wisconsin Fellowship of Poets Museletter*, "Daughter," under the title "Off the Record."

My appreciation to the poets who read drafts of these poems and offered helpful suggestions, including but certainly not limited to Erin Lyons, Karen Middleton, CJ Muchhala, Helen Padway, Mara Ptacek, Wendy Vardaman, and Phyllis Wax.

I owe additional thanks to poet, artist, and friend Wendy Vardaman for her insightful design of the book's cover.

Special thanks to Martha Collins for the example of her work, for her reading of an early version of this manuscript, and for our conversations about poetry and issues of race and racism.

The idea for this book originated in my happening upon a copy of *The Letters of Jessie Benton Frémont* edited by historians Pamela Herr and Mary Lee Spence. For their diligent work collecting and annotating the letters, I am grateful.

To publisher Jane L. Carman, for her commitment to innovative and inclusive poetry, for her energy and sense of fun, for her own poetry, my profound gratitude.

For Jeannette Martha, my mother, and her unfulfilled dream
of studying, teaching, and writing history

CONTENTS

I

The history should be considered as a skeleton, which is to be filled out by all the collateral information you can procure. Shakespeare's historical plays, and Scott's historical novels may be read to great advantage in connexion with the history of the period to which they belong.
> —*Young Lady's Friend*, by a Lady (Mrs. John Farrar)
> Boston, 1836

Manifest Destiny

is not my history,
not mine the brassy
territorial dreams.

I strum neither wistful
nor sassy chords for
ocean to ocean glory,
those songs put to rest
with fife and drum,
with ancestors long past.

I came into this world
a blank slate. Not mine
a dissonance of outdated
battles, though the blast at
Hiroshima rocked
the twice-painted cradle where,
placed on my tummy to sleep,
I'd wake face up and cry
until formula fed.

Now I live in a home near a lake,
on Wentworth Avenue, named
for one of the first white men
to stake a claim on Potawatomi
land here in Ouisconsin, as once
the name was quaintly spelled.

But what is this *bone dry*
history to me?

At the Worcester Art Museum
On viewing Willie Cole's *Kanaga Field Iron, 1997*

Stepping back, adjusting
my perspective I see an iron,
the supple upward curve of wood
the handle, the graceful spread of the base,

an iron of Brobdingnagian size.
What else does the base look like?
A boat. A boat turned upside
down. The hull of a boat.

Think about it. An iron of wood
would burn up. An inverted boat
would not sail. The Middle Passage,
enslaved domestic labor: facts of history.

This is how to redeem history
in art. Grab hold of it. Take care
that it not grab hold of you, sentence you
to long, complex clauses, multiple

subordinations. In Jessie's case,
the tin of rampant commas, the brass
of pedantic upper case and italics,
the quicksilver of weighty absences, silences.

Re-size it. Passage and apparent destiny.
Recast in your medium: dazzling rhetoric
into stanzas, mostly free verse;
iron history in the curve of wood.

History

Flat timeline
something to trip up
those who walk unawares

My mother longed to pick it up
but her father, her overbearing brothers
Somehow she puts it in my hands

I see a jump rope
turn it, turn another
double dutch

Let Me Not Misspeak

The Letters of Jessie Benton Frémont:
I open the book to her letter dated five years
after her marriage. On the page a voice pleading
with her husband, an undertone claiming my ear:

How old are you? You might tell me now I am
a Col.'s wife—won't you, old papa? Poor papa...

I read fiction fashioned out of Jessie's story.
The author, tone deaf, dedicates it to his wife
as if she were Jessie's shadow, he and Frémont
heroes, each she thus reduced to an

Immortal Wife.

I try to imagine a Capital girlhood,
daily guests for breakfast, for dinner,
a small table in a separate room
for children who misspeak.

Having misspoken she learns—
prompt others, reply briefly, smile.

I visit the archives where in Frémont's
grand leather-bound *Memoirs* her
introduction celebrates *the happy chance*
which made her the connecting link

in our manifest destiny

as if it were all glory, as if
there were no rifts between husband
and father, no indigenous people displaced,
no one lonely, hurt, hurting.

I touch the gold-leafed pages.
They impress but cannot convince
me. Between the fragile pages of father-
and husband-centered history,

I dig like crazy.

Jessie: Parsing Hegemony
    —St. Louis, September 1832

It ended much hard Indian warfare when
they at last captured Black Hawk. I saw him
when he was a prisoner at the Garrison—
a real Indian and real old warrior, captive but not subdued.

Case.   Gender.   Tense.
    Sauk.   Warrior.   Yes.

When Washington Irving was out there
a war-dance was held in the large council yard
that he might see real Indians at their real life.
I was very young, and the whole horrible thing,
as they grew excited, threw me into a panic.

Voice.   Number.
    Active.   Thrice-removed.

The Life of Ma-ka-tai-me-she-kia-kiak
told to Antoine LeClair, an interpreter, who,
not literate himself, not Sauk, told it
in frontier English to an editor J.P. Patterson,
who wrote it as he heard it,

as best as anyone hears anyone.

Wait. Did I hear correctly: *at last*
captured…captive but not subdued…
real Indians at their real life.
What is remembered
fifty-five years after the fact?

Mood   Person
   Indicative   First

I am afraid I did not study much.
Mere book-instruction was flat
and unprofitable to me after
my delightful home-teaching.

What did Blackhawk say? What did he look like?
Do the very young see true?
Do the very old?
Women? Men?

On St. Louis streets were priests and
Sisters of Charity in their special black dress
as well as French peasant women in
their thick white caps, sabots and full red petticoats
with big blue or yellow handkerchiefs crossed over the
     white bodices.
And with the Indians painted and blanketed gliding along
in files towards the enclosure around General Clarke's quarters
one would have been puzzled to say whose country it was now.

Jessie: The Bodisco Wedding, Georgetown, 1840
—it was April and December all through

Invited to his lavish Christmas parties
we children thought him Santa Claus.

Later I saw he *was a short and stout man*
with a broad Calmuck-face, much wrinkled.

At Miss English's Female Seminary
we saw his carriage pass through Georgetown,

that glitter of varnish and brasses and those
four prancing long-tailed black horses.

We did not see his whiskers, teeth, or manner,
did not see how money covers ugly.

He proposed marriage to our classmate,
a beauty the teachers would not allow us
to elect May queen. She was too poor.

But then with a wealth of show the wedding.

To the right of the bride was Mr. Buchanan,
tall and of fine presence and quite a type of Saxon
coloring and freshness despite his silvered head,

and with him, myself—aged fourteen.
We were allowed to be bride-maids
though too young to be in society—

The long white satin dress
—my first long dress—

all the belongings and duties
of my post of bride-maid
were made so many occasions
for teasing me with prophecies
that I would not return
to short frocks and lessons.

This vexed me, and to prove
I did not mean to be tempted
away from some years of study,
I cut off my hair close to the head.

Lt. Frémont: On First Meeting Jessie
—Washington City, 1841

I imagine you
your hair down, your dressing gown
without the library, without
pen and paper, ideas, words

I imagine you
your shoulders hunched
your face forward

a steaming cup of tea
your surprise at my quiet entry
your mouth, your quick
self-conscious smile

Jessie: How I Knew I Had a Choice

Roses still closely cupped and sturdy
geraniums sent to my mother—this fooled
no one. Perhaps Grandmother McDowell who

yesterday when their intense red brightened
the map-maker's room, watched only
the President's procession outside.

I looked at Mr. Frémont who waited
for the tea to settle, offered ices, bonbons
to all, yet kept an eye fixed on me.

My father missed nothing.

Sweet moment, sweet and savory,
red flowers, the red of blood, of a heartbeat, the heartbeat of color.

I lowered my eyes. I touched
my hair, not yet long enough
to stay up without a net.

His Story

John Charles Fremon
born Savanah, Georgia

son of Anne Beverly Whiting Pryor
who fled a forced marriage
and Jean Charles Fremon
the bold tutor who took chances

Called Charles Charley
Bastard

Pupil. Scholar. Expelled—
habitual irregularity
and incorrigible negligence

Called himself Fremont, adding the t
Frémont. C. Frémont, adding the accent
Instructor of mathematics, adding status
Surveyor. J. C. Frémont, adding initials

Learning his trade mapping Cherokee lands

Lieutenant J. C. Frémont, United States
Corps of Topographical Engineers
evening guest at the home of the powerful
Senator Thomas Hart Benton of Missouri

Confident beau. Husband. Leader
of western expeditions. Discoverer
of Christopher Carson   Kit   John
Carson   Frémont   Flag bearers

Explorer claiming Wind Mountain
with a flag he brings home and wraps
around Jessie   Father of Elizabeth
called Lily. Later Jessie writes her friend

Lizzie Blair Lee about *the paternal instinct,
a gift denied to Mr. Frémont.* Dictator
of his Rocky Mountain report to Jessie
John C. Frémont. Captain Frémont

The Pathfinder. Colonel Frémont
California Bear Flag Rebellion Frémont.
Court martialed Frémont. California gold
at his Mariposas mine, rich Frémont. Lucky
Frémont. Briefly California Senator Frémont

Republican Frémont. Candidate *Free Speech,
Free Press, Free Soil, Free Men, Frémont…
We'll give 'em Jessie* Frémont, but he can't
win Jessie's father's vote. He can't win

General Frémont. Civil War Commander
of the Western Department Frémont. Issuer
of a rogue emancipation proclamation Frémont
Inept, intractable Frémont. Dismissed Frémont

Gallant Frémont. Impulsive Frémont. Always
charming Frémont. Passionate Frémont
Railroad investor Frémont. Bankrupt Frémont
Jailed Frémont. Always a challenge Frémont

Arizona Governor Frémont. One term Frémont
Longing for the unexplored Frémont. New York
furnished rooms Frémont. Retired Frémont
Unfinished *Memoirs of My Life* Frémont

Frémont dead and buried. Reburied
with family, 3rd plateau, Rockland Cemetery
behind a moderate obelisk bearing his profile
and a medallion: *EXCELSIOR*

General Fremont
The
Pathfinder
1813 – 1890
inscribed on a mossy flat gravestone

Mr. Frémont Asks for Jessie's Hand

Here, this way. Let me
help you cross this muddy street.

Here to the side, away
from the splash of heavy carts.

Here is my arm, the crook of my elbow,
a place for you to rest your hand.

After being away, so far so long, now
here such a comfort, the light touch

of your gloved hand
here resting on my arm, oh,

Oh, here is your father.
Until tomorrow then.

Daughter

You don't want me to tell you about heat
but I'm going to tell you anyway

how the love of heat confines
courage to a slender summer

how alike, how different
heart and heat

how the heat of love may
lead to casting off modesty

how the heat of anger
closes into a fist
how tears of fury burn

how heat is not the same as warmth
how boiling hardens eggs, minutes, words
how untended fire may destroy the house

Jessie: Manifesto

The old frogs.
There were plenty of those,
powerful legs propelling them.

James Buchanan, the groomsman
I danced with when my friend married Bodisco,
both men old enough to be our fathers. Rumors
swirled that Buchanan asked Father for my hand.

Amphibians turned president, never presidential.
Perhaps there has never been a qualified president—
Little Van, slave-holding Tyler, Bleeding Kansas Pierce—
officious old men eying young girls. Lust.

I did not even know the word then.
Mr. Frémont, handsome, manly, never
volunteered his age, but when he took my hand
he looked young enough to be my father's son.

Jessie: My Dear Lizzie

Elizabeth Blair Lee,
because our fathers think alike,
because we're alike yet different,
because we're close as sisters,
because your quiet invites my voice,
because I never said so much about myself
to anyone but you before.

At the Archives

I read school catalogs. Campaign pamphlets.
Cartoons. Popular magazines. Newspapers.
Advice, lists, humor, editorials.

Congressional speeches: background
facts, extravagant praise, skillful
concessions, biting satire, caricature,

long balanced, rhythmic sentences,
quick left jab of understated insult,
the cause, the effect, the reiteration.

Documents covered in faded blue-grey
or tan-yellow paper. Hand-stitched binding,
resilient thread. Or perfect bound and
crumbling.

Pages thin as dust
dust, maybe mold: sneeze.

Sneeze: quick intake of something in the air
the body can't yet process

Why Jessie?

I opened a book
(and she spoke to me)

She claims happy,
her story all swans

(zoom in to cut context
zoom out to hide detail)

She may want a private pond,
placid white birds unruffled,

(all wings clipped, all plotting
shushed, all hurt in parentheses)

a smooth surface, the work
to stay afloat done out of sight

(freed to work on wages, but retained
in the same quarters, nearly as invisible,

her grandfather's body-servant Ralph,
her mother's nurse from childhood Sarah,
Old Harriot, Harriot's daughter, young Harriot)

I feel an understory stirring, churning.
I follow the tangled plots

across a continent of
pestiferous questions.

II

Joel Poinsett. Jessie Benton. Now Kit Carson. When it came to chance meetings that make careers, no man in American history was as lucky as John Charles Frémont.

—Martin Naparsteck, *Sex and Manifest Destiny*

History

It's an old story, strangely incomplete
when blood and thunder, the West was won
when Frémont mapped with gun, with Kit Carson
when lilacs last in the dooryard bloom'd
when men were manifestly men

I sing contrapuntal songs, those beneath
the stream of kitchen chatter, those
told before the snap of parlor fire
as if they make a difference
as if I could make a difference

Jessie's Destiny

Destiny is never manifest.
It's made out of words.

Destiny if it exists
gathers into cloud and fog,
grows dense, liquefies.

A word builder, her father,
catches the rain, freezes it.

She's quick, as they say, for a girl,
helps her father piece sentences together.
Destiny writ large, large
enough for John to read.

He's quick, too. Before she parses it,
he names the inchoate swirl she feels,
love,

marries her, marries it.

What Lizzie Blair Lee Doesn't Tell Jessie

Be as small as you can be.

As you turn the corner out of school-
girl tall, know that only the rare and proud
teacher hands you imaginary flowers.

You think your admirers attracted
to your wit, skill, grace, your height. They
are smitten with the challenge, the challenge

of cutting you down to size.

The most handsome, the most flattering,
the one who crooks his arm and tucks and pats
your hand in the fold of his elbow—that one—

you choose.

He'll tuck you into his baggage.
You'll conform to this shape

as if this is all your height was meant to be.

That ambitious amphibian that vexed you,
that frog about whom rumors swirled,
will not turn into a prince but
he is what you see. He may be
President. Consider him.

Jessie's Wedding, October 19, 1841

Her father's house, that door closed.
Her husband, not yet her husband.
Her way along the street, never more alone.
Her head, never more voices, their words tangled
promise me wait *marry me now* later *promise.*

Promise me.

Notice his grave eyes. See him as she, a school girl, did,
in the glorious light streaming through the windows,
western sun angling in on him, like grace. Read
the confidence in his stride, his spare elegance.
Assured, almost assured, another promotion,
his desire to build a great nation, from sea to sea.

His desire.

His reasons for their marriage, he said, found *a cold
and dull ear that heard but did not listen.* Her father.

She knew her father, his story of his six year courtship
of her mother. She knew her father had dreams for her,
had fears.
Look, he told her, comedy is patient. Viola waited, waited
for Orsino. Hurry leads to tragedy. A moment of thrill,
a life of regret. Consider Desdemona. Juliet.
Your future, talent, great promise is all I think of.

What future?

We do not have a moment to spare.
Do you John Charles…
The fire in his eyes.
Do you Jessie Ann…
Her head aches with joy.

Jessie: Brilliant Night

We walked out into the autumn chill, changed
as if we had crossed more than muddy lanes,
the hem of my dress unsoiled, the way a blur.
Soon, Love, soon. Mr. Frémont's words

floated with me back to my C Street home.
Inside all doors were sweetly closed,
mercifully closed. Father going over notes
for a speech. Mother, my sisters' hushed tones.

I dismissed Harriot after she helped me
brush my hair. I opened the window to see
the stars. Mr. Frémont knew how to plot
them, to calculate position. Mr. Frémont.

John. Mr. Frémont. Mrs. Mrs. Frémont.
I was sure we'd be all right. *Soon.*

Jessie: Bound
We have found the fountain of eternal youth for love
　　　　　—Jessie Benton Frémont

Banished from Father's house,
I brought a precious few things—
dresses, a necklace or two, my ring,
a dressing gown, comb, brush, and mirror,

my love-filled and sorrowing heart

to Mr. Frémont's lodgings,
to his narrow bed,
so that now what Hamlet said
seems what we were, that is,

bounded in a nutshell,

but then we never, I never, thought so,
for our dreams were vast as this land.
I counted him not *king* but us
grand freeholders *of infinite space.*

Jessie: Maternal Line

Father, they said, was indomitable, but Mother
in those young days still had her ways. Mother
oversaw our welcome back to C Street. Mother,

Elizabeth McDowell Benton. Had she as a child
been Betty? Eliza? Lizzie? No matter.
Mother mattered.

Then Father secured the lead for Mr. Frémont
of the Rocky Mountain expedition. Brilliant!
From his own hearth had gone forth the one

who carried his hopes to fullest execution. Mother
lived the years of opposition to Father's dream of Oregon
as American. Mother also concluded out of mere air

slavery mattered in ways her soul could not abide.
Willed slaves, Mother had the will to free them.
She set the tone for her brother, for her husband, my father,

Mother's word the path they followed. Emancipation.

I am Jessie Ann. My name admits no abbreviation.
Named for my father's father and my paternal uncle,
I am the long shadow of my mother,

strong will from strong, though bled, will.
I will proclaim my name, will dare
anyone, woman or man, to cross it.

I will make my way in terms so polite Miss English
will say her tedious lessons not lost. Like Mother,
I will create paths with my words.

Jessie: After the First Expedition, 1842

When Mr. Frémont returned and set about the task
of writing his report, he found that his pen could not
keep up the pace of his mind. I proposed a solution

to which he eagerly assented. Each morning
after tea or coffee we went at the work, he dictating,
I transcribing, allowing no interruptions till

our noon breakfast after which we'd work again,
details so flowing into bright sentences we had
to be called to dinner where that day's stories graced
also our table. These were the happiest hours of my life.

Jessie: Happiest Hours, But Then

My splendid health never failed me
with child months alone. Mr. Frémont
did not fail, returned home. Lily
arrived days after her dauntless
father. He had claimed the highest
Rockies peak and spread that same *wind-
whipt flag*, over us. Triumphant
time. More acclaim for the printed
report I wrote from Mr. Frémont's
spoken word, purpose-driven days,
our best—family, work, jointly
done. But then five of our first eight
years I face more lonely waiting
for his return, my heart aching.

Jessie: During the Second Frémont Expedition, 1845

Chief Justice Taney called at the little breakfast
hour. He had not been expected. He would want
his hearty hunting meal, hominy and ribs.

No longer a child who assumes all food grows ready
to be served, I slipped out to the kitchen, didn't expect
Old Harriot to be so cross. *Miss Jessie, ribs? Now?*

The Mister Justice will have to wait. Grits
are ready enough. I will get them to table.

So they had food to discuss. Father
took only bread and fruit with his coffee.
They started up again: what's good

for too much phlegm, for the vapors, their wives'
fragile health, what apothecary, what doctor, what
water, when to bathe and where, how to avoid drafts

how to cure a cold and how to avoid catching one.
Having had consumption as a youth, Father
devised and adhered to a regimen for himself.

Father had strong opinions
the Chief Justice did not share.

Rather than argue the Constitution
the Congress, the territories, western
expansion, what with Mr. Frémont gone,

maybe in Oregon, maybe facing danger,
rather than argue, argue slavery again,

better for all at table they argue their food
and their cures.

Three Fifths Before, During, and After Dred Scott

Being the second son of a hard-
drinking man who believed in
primogeniture, all rights to the first- born,
Roger Brooke Taney did not waste time

in envy of Michael, his elder brother.
Put to read law with a practice at Annapolis,
he swallowed each property-bound word,
strictly held to Constitutional fractions.

Jessie: From California to Court-Martial
        —1846–1847

We rejoiced in the glory, Frémont commanding
California, Father's sea to sea dream and
the third Frémont expedition the means.

Then *manifest injustice*. General Kearny commanding
turned the bloodless victory
into a tale of mutiny.

The court-martial. President Polk, accepting
the guilty verdict, cancelled the penalty,
offered Colonel Frémont clemency

instead of dismissal. The Colonel believing
charges, trial, verdict, all unjust, resigned.
The child I carried arrived.

A dear child, we named him Benton, honoring
Father. But such the turmoil, the baby weak.

I grieve.

Jessie: Young Harriot's Destiny and Mine
          —New York, 1848

With her I would not be afraid.
She had been with me,
with our family,
since her birth.

Now her man rouses up a crowd.
Noise on the street, at our hotel door,
as if we'd kidnap and sell her.
She should know better.

She should tell him what she told me,
told us, *yes, I will go to California
with you*. But now her will fails her.
In the face of so many, her courage fails her.

Her man says, *Here she is free. You take her
to uncertain territory. South. Slavery is not
her destiny. We are to be married.
We are each other's destiny.*

In the midst of the clamor, Harriot stands
at his side, silent. When they go, she goes.
I face my fears. I am to travel without Father,
without Harriot, only this suddenly hired immigrant.

Something is not right about her,
and this very long distance ahead,
the uncertain meeting with Mr. Frémont.

His fourth expedition, from Missouri
to the Great Basin and on to San Francisco,
and I after days at sea to Panama, by some means
across that narrow land to still more sea.

Somehow another ship to another port, and
if his expedition succeeds, there we'll meet,
there we're to settle. After five of eight years apart.
California. I helped put into words his talk of it.
Still it is hard to imagine, especially without Harriot.

Thief

It was a comfort never to have strangers about one at home.
   —Jessie Benton Frémont *Souvenirs of Our Times*

Lily clings to me in an unwonted way.
Mere child, she seems aware how uncertain
our journey, how ill-bred this strange servant
whom I dismissed for the night. To allay

Lily's fears, I put her to bed myself.
Try as I will, I cannot sleep. A creak
of the door. Someone tiptoes in. I see
out of the corner of my eye her stealth.

Near breathless with fear I watch the servant
quietly open trunks, remove household
goods to her carryall and leave, as bold
a thief as ever I could imagine.

When I catch my breath, I rise, lock the door,
and ponder if this is the start, what more?

At Sea

I could not, of course, sleep again
or so, tossing and turning, I believed.
Young Harriot walked into the room

taller than I remembered her to be,
thinner, stiffer, advancing
without bending at the knee

without meeting my inquiring eye,
no smile or loving glance at Lily.
She threw herself across me

falling forward like a tree
I could not breathe, her weight
upon me, how heavy, cold, stony.

Somehow I loosed my arms
pushed to free myself, reached
out for her but grasped at empty air.

She had been a dream, a feverish dream.
I slept again but uneasily.

What's Lost to History

The name of young Harriot's fiancé
His place of residence and later theirs
His source of income, his and her employers

Their work organizing free people of color

How he and Harriot celebrate their marriage
If they have children and their names, birthdates
If they stay in New York and where buried
How they avoid bounty hunters and enslavers

What favorite foods, colors, jokes, songs
How deep their love for their mothers-in-law
whether present, passed, or sold down river
What chance, how much manifest courage and why
for their happily ever after

Jessie: California Must be Free

Help is offered at a price. I'll none of it.
Mother was right. There are other ways, better,
God-fearing ways. Even if I have to cook, clean,
sew for myself, nurse Baby Charley myself.

Help at a price. A price for the woman.

It was always there even when it was not there—
this slavery question seemed part of the landscape
like the gradual uphill slope of the road that appears flat
until you walk it on a hot day, baby sweaty in your arms.

Help at a price, a woman for sale.

I would as soon place my children
in the midst of smallpox, as rear them
under the influence of slavery.

Jessie: My Dear Lizzie

Because I wish I could be as good,
as ever outwardly calm as you
while ever as quick within.

Because you sense when
I *am all dammed up—for want
of sympathizing ears.*

At the Archives
Rule 2: Use book cradles at all times

No matter how I position myself,
no matter the angle of my camera,
given the abundant overhead lighting,
I cannot find a way to photograph
any of the documents I place
in the cradle on the table
without also catching
my shadow on the page.

Why Jessie?

Because she favors the simplest sentences
(though taught the rhetoric of intricate
verbal phrases, layered subordinate clauses)
when most vexed or resolute or forlorn, I check
in what agitated waters swim her syntactic swans.

Because she appears the seamlessly devoted wife
(servants picked up, patched, stitched what ripped)
yet between the rehearsed words, I see a gap wherein
sit an inner cross-hatching, conflicting emotions,
goals and frustrations, ideals and banalities.

Because she dared leave comfortable hearth
(learning of deceit, loss, thievery; catching
a dangerous Panama fever, waiting, waiting) I can
leave her neither in fiction nor in time-worn rhymes,
metronomic rhythms, four square lines.

Because at sea and in new territory she finds
new forms emerge, harden, subside, reshape, so I
(inspired by history rendered in Willie Cole's art)
let a series of sounds sometimes more quietly align,
let rhymes fly mid-line, sometimes out of sight.

III

The improper phrase, "freezing sarcasm." seems to be coming into use on both sides of the Atlantic. ... In English, the common and true meaning of sarcasm is biting, cutting, stinging, caustic speech. Sarcasm bites, and cuts, and stings, and burns, but it never freezes.

—The New York Ledger, 1875

Senator Thomas Benton: *It's Always Slavery*
    —1848

When an anti-slavery clause was attached
to the bill to create in Oregon
a territorial government,
I rose in protest.

Why raise again this question of slavery?
How does it alter our manifest destiny?

Remember Exodus, I said, the plague of frogs
You could not look upon the table but there were frogs,
you could not sit down at the banquet but there were frogs,
you could not go to the bridal couch and lift the sheets
but there were frogs!
So, too, with *this black question,*
forever on the table, on the nuptial coach,
everywhere!

Jessie: the Fifth Expedition, 1853

Four months
no word from Mr. Frémont.

Father, cold, unsympathetic.
He talks Kansas, only Kansas.
The Territory, divide it obliquely

as the rivers flow,
southeast from northwest.
Kansas, Kansas, three times Kansas.

He talks a mid-continent path for the railroad.
Our Pacific ports. We can, we must, expand.
He lost his Senate seat, his House seat, still talking

expansion westward. What he dare not say:
without expanding slavery.

Father, Father, they don't listen, won't listen.
You argued statehood the thirty years they ignored
Oregon, let British claims manifestly linger.

Now they want territory only because it is southern,
only because they want slaves.

Message from Mormon Country, 1853

Four months
no word from Mr. Frémont.

Then in the quiet, I hear him.
despite the distance.
He does not stammer.

His voice is dream-like,
but it is not a dream.
He says *we are safe.*

I hear him.
Three trapezoids or a rectangle,
what matters the shape of Kansas?

He journeyed as planned
through mountains beyond Kansas
to Utah through fierce winter snow.

Now clearly his voice, *Jessie.*
From across the continent
soft, loving to C Street.

He is warm.
He is alive.

Mr. Frémont: On Staying the Course, 1853

It was not exactly as I later wrote:

We were moving in fogs and clouds
through a region wholly unknown to us
and without guides

and were therefore obliged
to content ourselves
with the examination of a single line

and the ascertainment of the winter condition
of the country over which it passed
which was in fact the main object.

That single line actually uncertain.

After four months, after losing
our way, after eating our mules,
we found warmth in Parowan.

Alone in the quiet night,
I spoke her name, *Jessie.*
Then I spoke the truth.

I told her *we are safe.*

Jessie: Father at Work

Father helps seat Mother comfortably nearby,
fidgets in his own chair, dips his pen, writes:

In this description of the country I have relied
chiefly on Frémont, whose exploration,

directed by no authority,
connected with no company,
swayed by no interest—
wholly guided by himself,
and solely directed to the public good,

would be entitled to credit upon his own report,
unsupported by subsidiary evidence;
but he has not left the credit
of his report to his word alone.

He has done, besides, what no other explorer had done:
he has made the country report itself.

Besides determining elevations barometrically,
and fixing positions astronomically,
and measuring objects with a practiced eye—

besides all that, he applied the daguerreotype art
to the face of the wild domain,
and made it speak for itself.

Father imagines the roll of this rhetoric
bringing all who hear to support the noble cause:
a railroad that skirts the most pestiferous question,
binds together the union from eastern to western sea.

He remembers Mother's presence,
serves their tea.

Jessie: Father and Pestiferous Questions

Father stood firm on both his principles:
the union and national expansion
without slavery's expansion.

Thus he lost his Senate seat
amid *popular sovereignty* clamor,
ill-conceived and cunning rhetoric,

a mask to cover what Mother abhorred,
humans owning humans. Mother died
this year of Nebraska-Kansas.

Father seeks to stop the siren sound
of *popular sovereignty*, travels tirelessly,
delivers lecture after lecture to separate

the pestiferous question of freesoil
from the drawing of state boundaries.
Against his opponents' seductive slogan

the subtle sounds of his Latinate phrase
proved poor wax, neither stops up ears
nor sounds a more powerful drumbeat.

Even unnamed, especially unnamed,
slavery holds sway. Senator Atchison—
intolerable old bullfrog, his pompous air:

"Colonel Benton" argues apparently
for a certain division of territory into states
and for the building of a railroad on a central route,
but...

He has led the very 'pestiferous' host
which he pretended to fear.
He has become the commander
of the 'pestiferous freesoil' opposition.

What a swirl of words Atchison heaves
onto the land. From sea to sea we stagger.
His the thunder and the storm. Nebraska. Kansas.
The tempest now churning will not be averted.

Jessie: Fire Upon Fire, 1851–1855

Let me tell you about heat. I learned.
Two San Francisco homes lost to fire.
Oppressive heat up at our Mariposas mine—

Indians, bears & miners…very out of the way—

Yet gold drew even more men. They assailed our claim.
Mr. Frémont remained there lest tensions boil over.
I craved society, a proper home. Home? where?

Washington City now itself oppressive

given the loss of Father's place in Congress.
It was like a cooling sea air when
Chief Justice Taney himself read

the Supreme Court decision in our favor,

in favor of our Mariposas claim—
it was much spoken of as evidence
of his kind feelings to us.

Nevertheless a smoldering sense of loss.

We mourned Mother. We grieved
yet for our little Anne Beverly
though already I was with child again.

And more.

At C Street *my father's house*
was destroyed by fire, and with it
seemed to go the old life which had been
so full and complete and delightful.

Frémont Fever, the 1856 Presidential Election
Free Speech, Free Press, Free Soil, Free Men, Frémont and Victory

He made the far west seem within reach.
He marked spaces for unsettling dreams.
He found his name stamped across the land
Frémont streets, towns, cities, counties.

Rutherford B. Hayes, then nationally unknown,
a young Ohio lawyer, found Fremont the solution
for one of three Ohio towns, all called Sandusky
and thus began Hayes' rise as resolver of an impasse.

When the Frémont name reached east to west,
that stretch of acclaim, it became tender.
What to such currency is a court martial,
a retreat from public life, a fourth and fifth

expedition largely unsuccessful? The *Pathfinder*
would carry the new party to power, might
carry it to the President's house, carry there,
carry to the nation, freesoil principles,

As Republicans Prepare to Nominate Frémont
      Speech of Hon. Charles Sumner in the Senate of the United
      States, 19th and 20th May, 1856

The Nebraska Kansas act was,
said the honorable senator from Massachusetts
in every respect a swindle.

Sir, it was a swindle of God-given inalienable rights.
Turn it over, look at it on all sides, and it is everywhere
a swindle; and, if the word I now employ has not the authority
of classical usage, it has, on this occasion, the indubitable
authority of fitness. No other word will adequately express
the mingled meanness and wickedness of the cheat.

His words rang out across the land, stirred the Blairs to join
with Republicans pushing the nomination of Frémont
for President.

His words carried up the eastern seaboard to Jessie's retreat,
and reverberated loudly through both Houses of Congress.

South Carolina Representative Preston Smith Brooks
heard endless talk of Sumner's words,
read the speech himself in its unrelenting entirety,
grasped his cane in hand, made his way to the Senate
Chamber, to Senator Sumner's desk, where he raised that cane,
raised it and lowered it with pitiless force again
and again, on the head, the back, the arms
of the man whose words offended him, right there
in the hallowed hall of democracy where, oh help us,
no one could, no one dare, stop him.

Senator Benton: Frémont Cannot Win My Vote

And with Father this is only the expression
of years of distrust of Mr. Frémont's judgment
        —Jessie Benton Frémont, April 1856

I wanted better for her
not flash of wild promise
no more enduring than the bloom
of morning glory, day lily

She danced with Buchanan.
The throng of match-making matrons
thought him Washington City's most
eligible bachelor. He never married.

Did he long for Jessie,
his match at the Bodisco wedding, but only
as first bride-maid to first groomsman.
Why not a next step for them, when
she would be of age, to the altar?

All the virtues of an envoy,
all the skill of Congress, all the future
as clearly manifest as the enduring rose.
She'd so grace the president's house.

My colleague, nearly my age, true,
but not as ostentatious as Bodisco, husband
of the poor school girl she championed,
Buchanan neither so old nor so ungainly,

What is it about him?
What is it about her?

Jessie: The Campaign Sings Jessie

Chorus: *It's time to be doing, the play has begun,*
There's mischief a brewing, as sure as a gun;
The Buck and the Breck noodles are stupidly bent
On choosing a Bach for our next President.

A *Bach*. A bachelor. *Buck* Buchanan, Buchanan again.
Fifteen years later and I've a daughter near grown.
They think I'll be flattered. They think I don't know
the code among men. But I lived frontiers beyond society.

A bachelor, who, like his species, you know,
Is afraid of the girls, and to union a foe;
Then up and be doing, for danger is rife,—
A man is but moonshine who hasn't a wife.

I who knew not the words then know now
what they imply in their rhymes.

Just think what queer things his receptions must be—
Uncouth gander parties, as all must agree;
For a house with no mistress a place is, I ween,
Where no well-bred lady would wish to be seen.

Mr. Frémont says nothing even
after the singing outside our hotel.
It is not his way to speak easily.
He seems inattentive even to advice
from those closest to his cause.

She's wise and she's prudent; she's good as she's bonnie
For Virtue n Valor she takes a brave stand:
For the Chieftain's White Mansion she's better than onie
So give her 'God speed!' there, the flower of the land.

Let them sing; *the play has begun,*
I know more than Hamlet's Ophelia
how to play a part in this intrigue.
Father at his best taught me.
Embrace the sunshine. Ignore the ghost.

Waking During the Campaign

This cannot be my dream.
Calm   Exhale
How so this vision in my sleep?
Expel this vapor. Exhale.

I do not know
the man, the woman bent low
over a candle. Beneath
the table, their feet bare.

That man, no, no,
too tall for Mr. Frémont, no.
Never.

I've never seen that sparsely furnished room
nor been held so in a whisper, would never
allow knit stockings to lie carelessly
on the floor. Never so careless of dress.

How so in my dream? What woman?
Impossible. Mr. Frémont stays home
out of the public eye
as proper candidates do.

Yet so chilling. As if I suffered
one humor or another too much.
If Mother were still with us,
she'd have me bled.

Slow   Calm   No alarm
Fluff pillows myself
Catch my breath Slow

Breathe   Out   Full   Fully
Can't be. No. He would never….
I must go back to sleep.

Why John Leaves Home

To find paths
To follow a passion
or cool one
To sleep outdoors

Because of trout- teeming rivers
Because of the succulence of elk
Because of stars in night skies
Because nothing at home engages him

It offers purpose
It offers titles: Lieutenant, Captain
It frees men from titles: Frémont, Carson
It frees men to walk, ride, navigate,

scale real
rather than
imagined heights
It frees men

even if it means cold
even if it means hunger
even if it opens the mind
so that it suffers when closed again

closed in a court-martial
closed in dinners free of discordant topics
closed in a presidential campaign
closed in by, clothed in, wifely competence

Closed in.
Every night foggy dreams.
Every day, everywhere
a coffin.

Jessie: Unbent

I wake again
again in the dark

Oh, for the dreamless sleep
of chloroform during childbirth

Instead loss upon loss: Father's affection,
Mr. Frémont's attention, the election

to Buchanan, but think
how his the greater loss, his dignity
bent to the southern will,

his life public and empty.

Yesterday on the train, a widow
and her children, resolute, going
to her sister who'll provide for them.

Brave example!

My sister, her husband, in France,
will welcome me into their society.

Maybe together our family to New York
or California, our gold mine, claim secured.

And, joy, my dear Lizzie Blair Lee
at last to be a mother.

Not to be lost: my courage.

Jessie: My Dear Lizzie

Because your letters make me feel at ease again
after crossing Panama, after Chagres fever, after
the San Francisco fire, after *I really have*
something like the blues

Because you opened your Silver Spring home to me,
to my frail Paris-born daughter Anne Beverly,
who did not survive

At the Archives
After viewing "Manifest Destiny,"
Abraham Solomon's 1857 Engraving

Is destiny in the house,
on the table, in the cards,
in the teller? In the Cupid
grounded beneath the table?

Or is destiny outside already
composed one-third open sky,
one-third billowing cloud,
one-third tilled field and virgin forest?

Among these women
is there a Jessie?
Not she who,
glassy-eyed, swoons.

Perhaps she who offers a shoulder,
whose ringed fingers stay her sister's hand.
Or she who shuffles the cards, lays, reads
and interprets them. She may not be

in the picture at all but like us a viewer
who wonders what connects
landscape with parlor game,
feminine subjects with political title

and where in this manifest
destiny are the men?

Why Jessie?

Because all the roles his women played partially fit,
but because no Shakespearean role fit her completely,
she invents plots that rewrite her tragedies.

Because Lieutenant Frémont's stories whet
her school girl appetite for an adventurous life,
romance that's challenged when she's his wife.

Because she briefly seems a happier Juliet
hurried to the altar though her parents disapprove
his class, his uncertain family, rumors of his earlier loves.

Because though not shrewish, yet
as a girl she was as iron-willed as Kate
and as a new wife seemed equally tamed.

Because like Portia when her plans are upset,
she splices words to achieve her goals,
and plays what are considered masculine roles.

Because how unforgettable her ability to forget
the rifts and write herself into history as *the link*
by which husband and father *became one in the work*

of opening out our Western country to
emigration, a claim both false and true.

IV

Now changed the scene, and changed the eyes
That here once looked at glowing skies,
Where Summer smiled;
Where riven trees and wind-swept plain
Now show the Winter's dread domain—
Its fury wild.
—John C. Frémont

Jessie: The President Must Listen to Me

Father lived and breathed history. He took to heart its wars, its issues, saw
how generals, statesmen, heroes stood strong, saw how their winning
or losing rolled forward to our own times. He taught me.

Tonight, with the moon's glare on the dressing table mirror, I cannot even
see myself, not clearly. So much unseen, even in full sun, unseen by
friends, old friends, once friends, unseen by men who cannot look at
themselves in the mirror, can no longer look me in the eye.

Frank Blair.

Father so kind to him. Father offered Frank his connections. How else does
a man like Frank, fond as he is of drink, gain election to Congress?

I cannot see why he turns against me. Against us. Can he not see the soldiers
in tattered uniforms, some with no uniforms, some even without
shoes? His friends sell the army blind horses, sick mules, rancid meat,
thin or rent canvas for tents. Troops muster in, muster out. Unpaid.
Discharged. How the greedy love war! The money to be made.

Can they not see? Such an ill-equipped army cannot win this necessary war.
Why do they not see how order is necessary? How General Frémont
must be obeyed? The chain of command is only as strong as its weak-
est link. This army, so many weak links up and down the chain.

The great cause of this war, emancipation, they do not, cannot, will not see.
They refuse to see how it rallies new volunteers despite the cold, the
need to bring their own guns and horses, even their own food. This
war will be won only if we fight for a great cause.

This mirror, the moon. I want to see myself clearly. I will be seen.

I will tell what I see. Officers duck, dodge, shun, evade responsibility. They say General Frémont's Guard too showy. They say his style too aloof, they disregard his orders. They mock him. They show no will to win. They seem not to care. They want the General replaced.

I will, I must, to Washington City. The President must see me, must listen, must know why the General's order must stand, why we must emancipate the secessionists' slaves.

General Jessie, they call me.
Why do they hate us?
Why do they hate me?

Jessie: After the President Will Not Listen
Compiling *The Story of the Guard*

Trust not the Blairs.
Trust is the first victim
of war. Friendships die.
Friend against friend.

Only Zagonyi's men, the General's
valiant German Guard, trustworthy.
This is not the St. Louis I know.
I knew, I knew well. Father,
my family, here before any Blairs.

The Guard, these loyal men.
Frank Blair not to be trusted.
What reports did he feed Lincoln?
Montgomery Blair, US Postmaster,
Lincoln's confidant. Mail not secure.
No way to build an army.

They do not understand how difficult.
They do not understand how we are without.
They do not understand how brave these men.
They send us blind mules, lame horses,
ripped tents, ill-sewn uniforms, spoiled beef.
These agents put in their own pockets soldiers' pay.
No support.

Frank, so sly, deserves arrest, undermining
the General at Springfield, a victory,
Major Zagonyi's Guard on the verge
of another beyond Springfield,
but dismissed. Without pay.
General Frémont dismissed, they say,
for issuing an emancipation order without

approval. All up the chain of command
they do not want this war to be about slavery
as if that is not exactly what it is about.

Secession. Bold in St. Louis.
The Blairs insufferable.
Loyalty dismissed. The elite Guard—
their enlistment called irregular,
their pensions denied.
I must tell their story.
It's already in the documents.
People will listen.
The Story of the Guard.
If people only knew.

What Lizzie Blair Lee Writes to her Husband
    —October 14, 1861

I heard today that Frémont
has been outgeneraled
and is soon be replaced.

Jessies part in this matter
has disappointed me sorely—

Things which I had learnt
to believe about her husband
made me think him unreliable—

but only added to my pity
& affection for her—
I am now convinced

that in countenancing
& covering his sins
she has shared

& been degraded by them—

& yet I can see in her efforts
to elevate him & excite his ambition
a struggle to win him from his gravelling nature—

What Jessie Does Not Say to Lizzie Blair Lee

We were never friends
though I feel indebted to you, your invitation
to Silver Spring when my little Anne was dying,
though our fathers are, were, may have been.

In Washington City people useful to you
are called friends. How useful Mr. Frémont's

fame to establish the Republican party.

If he had won the presidency what power
as backroom advisors for your father,
your elder brother, now Postmaster General,
the younger, sometime office-holder in Missouri.

But Blairs always win, always build
their power, will inform on old friends
to the President, work at cross purposes
even with the war which must be won.

I know how you are going
to gesture before you lift your left hand
upturned to your waist, more claw than fist.
Remain silent. Do not trouble yourself

to muster up words. I will not hear you.

On the Edge

What to do when dream after dream dissipates
like morning fog in dazzling autumn sun?
Can you hold on to spring when the blossom's done?

Or hold the green of summer on the chance
the New York manor got with western gold
may sustain you as you resign to growing old?

Can you still prove brilliant? Bright
as the swoop of scarlet edging the oak
growing in the brisk air bold,

bold as an experienced lover, or a thief
while the household sleeps?

Jessie: Moving Down

Things I did not put up for auction,
things that would not have sold if I had,
things too small, too cheap, to have made
a difference if they had sold:

Charley's marbles. When he lost sight of them
given first his own pony, later a boat, he lost
sight of how like a self-contained world they are,
each its own untroubled, inviolable design.

Lily's jump rope. Solitary jumper. She never
had friends who would turn for her, and she
for them. At first at Mariposas some friends
despite her stammer.
                              Then the campaign
and fame kept neighbors away. We moved
and moved again and again. Washington City,
France, Pocaho up here on the Hudson.

Now again.
Surely in the rented New York rooms
some space for these cheap little things.
These and the two swaddle blankets,
second-born Benton's, Paris-born Anne's.

They no longer suffer.

In Rented Quarters
we outlast so much—even ourselves
      —Jessie Benton Frémont

She married for love
thinking the warmth of her hearth
enough, enough to keep it steady,
steady burning, flourishing, at home

Love grew
comfortable: welcomed, feted, celebrated, too
comfortable. Limited. Confined.

She married for love
but her lover went forth, exploring,
as if love knows no bounds, as if, patient,
it could wait and, waiting, wanting, grow stronger.

Oh, well, she married for love
not convenience, though she could not hear
what her mother tried to tell her: love
may be a rough sea journey, or
an overland passage to an uncertain destination.

She married for LOVE!
and found herself wanting,
wanting her husband to meet her
where he had said, a welcoming new state,
wanting her old confidence, her sense of knowing,
leading, inspiring, creating the way.

She married for love and instead got money,
a motherlode of gold, to buy, build, furnish a home
in California, another in New York, as if the fire
of the first hearth could be replaced,
and any warmth would suffice.

She married for love and then the money, too
was gone, the good name extinguished, the homes sold
the quarters rented, the rooms too small
to hold their life together.

She married for love, and she had five children:
a daughter who cared for her to the end, two sons
with wives and lives, struggles of their own,
a son and a daughter who didn't survive.

She married for love, and in the end she got charity,
not exactly the love she thought she married.

A Note Jessie Would Have Burned

It doesn't hurt any more,

his stubborn silence, his
exasperated turn of head, of body
angled away from me, my questioning not

his opinion, his
right to that opinion, but simply how,
why, what reasons, so I could understand

his holding fast, his cold eye, his
chilly back as if any doubt were disloyal
and his wife should be in step

never mind abrupt turns
of thought and of fortune.
It doesn't hurt anymore.

I write those words and I
mean them. Was there ever anything
as wonderful as writing away the night?

I write even when I
doubt words, when the night is
distant clouds against distant sky.

I write dark against dark. I
am the night sun moving in smooth
uncounted hours, the past becoming a place

I write. I
free myself from time.

I am winter, I am
a single oak. Everything
else is snow, white
without giving light.

Writing a Way

After the war in which her husband served
     briefly as Union commander of the Western Department,
after an exhausting trip to argue her husband's case with Lincoln,
after he looks askance at her travel-dusty dress, her disordered hair,
after he dismisses her, after he relieves her husband of his command,
after he dies, after the war,
after their sojourn in Europe
after her husband's failed investments
     put their Hudson River estate, their yacht,
     the stable, all the paintings, rugs, books up for auction
after Lizzy Blair Lee visits her in her rented rooms
after she feels the bite of being poor, the sting of being pitied,

Jessie sees a way.
She will sell what she still owns,
     her stories.

Composing Herself

Like most writers, Jessie begins,
Jessie begins with a disclaimer:

I don't know how to do this.

She begins panoramically,
five subjects, somewhat related,
three or four sentences each.

Jessie begins
doubting herself,
doubting this project,

how cheap, how vulgar, how unworthy,
how like the taste of sour milk
to identify herself in terms of others,

those she had the good fortune to know
when she had good fortune.

She begins to vanquish doubt.
She cannot afford it.

She begins to focus,
to find the word to open
for Martin Van Buren, let's say.

She considers how to say this,
his love of young people, no. His sons grown
he liked to gather other young people about him.

She begins
subtly to shift from assigned topic
Distinguished People I Have Known

to the real one, the Bodisco wedding, the teasing
that Buchanan was charmed, would seek her hand,
how this *vexed* her, how she blunt cut her hair

how she then eloped with Mr. Frémont
before my hair was long enough
to stay up without a net

She learns sleight of hand
how to tuck into the middle
what might frighten reader, subject,

or herself.

She learns how to evade naming offenses
from which the country has not yet healed.
About the beating in the Senate of Charles Sumner,

Jessie writes of visiting him *when he was very ill*
as if this injury were an infectious disease.

Though Grandmother Benton
told her sewing hurts your chest,
and though she hates to sew,

hates thimble, needle, thread, scissors,
she learns to cut and seam together
the pieces chance provides

—here, now, red geraniums in the window box
    cut them from life, stitch them in pen onto the scene
    in the dining room of Father's house before it burned,

and thus her frock takes shape.

She begins to include dialogue
to add flashback to convey depth,
to alter, to mend, to measure

her words to fit the style
of the patron. It is a hard lesson,

this writing. Jessie the editor,
Jessie the compiler,
begins to learn
to write in her own voice.

What is a poor woman to do?
And she begins to find
it also brings her pleasure.

After Reconstruction

Only then will Rutherford Hayes
find in Arizona a place for Frémont
and only after his wife, a Jessie fan, recalls
for Hayes his early celebration of Frémont's name.

Jessie: Teaching History in Arizona

My last best memory of Governor Frémont—
a visit to the Prescott school, where he
delighted the children, keen students
of mathematics and science.
                                    But of history,
they complained how dull, pointless. He smiled,
turned, extended his hand to touch mine. *Not
so, not in Mrs. Frémont's charming style,*
he said, his voice a warm embrace.
                                    I thought
how tender. I felt hopeful as a bride
soon to be settled in a happy home.
I told stories as I heard them from my
father, alive beyond *old books and dry bones*

But soon history was not enough. Again
frontier lonely, again deserts of men.

John: Memoirs of My Life

Jessie, you in California, hear me.
Did you ever read, read carefully
the closing words I actually
wrote myself?
                    Manifest destiny—
for shame, always linked to slavery.
The pristine west, its rugged beauty
all that I loved, streams, mountains, valleys
I mapped and measured, guaranteeing
they would be crossed, sullied.
                              Irony!
Yes, what is conquered is lost. For me
double irony. From *grand and lovely*
features of nature, note this, Jessie,
into the poisoned atmosphere, treachery
of politics,
          and I not nearly so mean.

John Without Jessie
New York 1890

No more sentences.
No adjustments for tone,
for rhetorical effect.
No metaphors.

My age? 77 years.

What signifies: a throaty hum,
low, already deeper than pain.
Her name without its sibilants.
Admitting loss.

American Exceptionalism

John, it is said, selected the site
wild and free as any he'd seen,

where he'd be buried, in position
to overlook the Hudson, its wide

run upriver from the port, from the story
of our country's exceptional history

already in his time approaching conclusion
already regression toward the mean.

No Mention of Lily? What Else Forgotten?
Letter from Jessie Benton Frémont to Lucy Keeler,
Los Angeles, July 18, 1899

I have
had a singularly happy
life—happy in the loving
friendship of my Father—
of my husband—
of my two sons, and
now of my dear
and fine grandson.

Other things are clouds
only—but behind them
shines steady and splendid
the one lasting thing, home-love.

Jessie's Happiness

Judge Black of Pennsylvania, who had a rough wit but a kind nature,
said once to me, "Your geese are all swans."

You could say it's a fiction.
You could say it's a rhetorical strategy.
Or her memory failing her,
but as a principle of epistemological

investigation, let's say she knows
more than historians and poets can guess.

What is it to be happy? What is supposed?
That it is a flat line, being free of trouble?
If so, then indeed is death
entry to the kingdom of heaven.

Is it the exhilaration of success?
Many beaux seeking to dance with you,
you, the envy of the shy, women and men?
You hosting salons, bringing others acclaim?

Or is it like democracy, messy—
raucous throngs claiming clashing principles?
Scrappy? Elbow, smile, charm, sweep your way in—
Gather your calm. Find your rhythm, pitch, pace,

parsing not each word in prescribed sentences
but finding the part of speech, case, gender,
mood, number to construct the voice
for the truth as you will have it known.
You, the pathmaker. You the mythmaker.

Where Now, Jessie?

Cherry Grove, near Lexington, Virginia,
where you were born, where
Grandmother McDowell said better
marry into an old house than a new?

St. Louis, still a French village
when your father arrived, when you
walked to an easygoing school, when
a girl, you saw Blackhawk chained?

St. Louis of the Civil War, undersupplied,
understaffed, headquartered in a Benton home.
General Frémont, Commander a mere 100 days,
Blair treachery and/or Frémont incompetence?

Bear Valley, the unbearable heat and the hotly
contested Mariposas claim that brought you
and Mr. Frémont gold, your claim upheld
by your C Street guest Chief Justice Taney?

Pocaho on the Hudson bought with California gold?
How splendid, how spacious for the children, how
lost—Mr. Frémont's inept investments—how
painful the auction, how dreary the rented rooms.

C Street where your mother was bled,
where after going free soil Republican, where
after Mr. Frémont's anti-slavery presidential bid,
the door closed to you, the air chilled?

Where years earlier a place was set
in a small side room for those who
brought disruption to the dinner table,
where later precious papers lost in fire?

Still crisscrossing the continent?
Have you stopped talking to me?
Still searching?

What's History to Me
   I stand in front of a quiet Blair House,
   Pennsylvania Avenue, Washington DC, January 2017

History is a meandering river, different
from the line that represents it on a map.
See a meeting of streams, the placid
Ohio giving way to the muddy Mississippi,
already conjoined with the Missouri.

Those who don't know history
are destined to repeat…. Repeat:
those who know history see exactly
how we live on its flood plain.

The 19th century is a Congressional sentence in Senator
Benton's grand oratorical style that can chain you unsuspecting
in its hold: 64 words, three clauses, thirteen prepositional
phrases, six verbal phrases, a style as schoolroom popular,
as lecture hall eloquent, as church and courtroom erudite as
Lynley Murray's *Grammar*. Whitman sometimes with, mostly
against its grain, self-publishes, Dickinson slants the rhymed
quatrain and can't publish, Twain begins *American* literature
ungrammatically rafting down the river.

As we live and breathe we know
what happens to us is chancy,
what happened inevitable
only because it now seems over.

But for Thomas's persistence, Jessie might not be.
But for his orphaned mother's wild flight from
a forced marriage to no marriage, no John Charles.

And here we are.

John Charles Frémont clouds his reputation, Jessie cultivates a geranium-shaded myth. There are no schools named after Chief Justice Taney, only the haunting invisible school of thought we pretend has disappeared. History carries us down river. Oregon could have been another country. Kansas could be the shape of Vermont. Times three. Given the choice of John Charles Frémont, James Buchanan, and Millard Fillmore, who would you pick? Such choices. Such chances. Lizzie Blair Lee reveals her deepest thoughts only to her dear husband,

and here on an ephemeral pond we are
in the midst of statements,
misstatements, restatements,
additions, admissions, emotions,
omissions, deletions, shadows,
empty words, burning words,
like a dream deferred
with all deliberate speed.

Turn Up the Volume.

I can't breathe.
I can't sleep.
I have a dream.

My Last Day at the Archives

I read Jessie's *California Sketches*.
Her nearest neighbors at Mariposas, the Crawfords,
gathered gold trailings in the stream only occasionally,
only occasionally tended their garden, their cabin.

Despite their sloth, how haughty they are with Burke
and Isaac, she says, as if their arrogant white
is worth more than these good men's color.

The Indian women who carry her loads
of laundry downhill to the spring, she says,
are very pretty when they wear calico, freshly pressed.

She also says she taught them to be steady.
She pays each one at the day's end so,
needing more, they will return the next day.

Seeing offensive white privilege in others may
or may not open an inwardly critical eye.

Early the next morning I thank and count out a tip
for my turbaned taxi driver who arrives on time,
and I enter Worcester's Union Station just
as the homeless are being swept out.

Then from Boston all the way home,
working every food court, with every
broom, many keys, many carts, people
no longer invisible; no longer invisible

one of the pilots, two flight attendants,
two first class passengers,
one couple with an infant,
one tall young backpacker,

and the rest of us on this trip are white.

Why Jessie?

In 2009 double dutch
became a varsity sport
in New York public schools

It requires at least three
two to turn the rope
one (or more) to jump

History is a time line
Those who do not know history
leave it lying underfoot

We trip on it again and again

TIMELINE OF KEY EVENTS

1787   Northwest Ordinance passed by Congress to establish
                a procedure for admitting new states to the Union on
                equal terms with the original thirteen. Article six out-
                lawed slavery in the states to be formed. Ohio, Indiana,
                Illinois, Michigan, and Wisconsin were admitted to the
                Union under its provisions.

January 21, 1813   Birth of John Charles Frémont to Anne Beverly Whit-
                   ing Pryor and Jean Charles Fremon in Savannah, Geor-
                   gia.

1820   The Missouri Compromise undermined the anti-slav-
                ery provision of the Northwest Ordinance by allowing
                Missouri to enter the Union as a slave state.

May 31, 1824   Birth of Jessie Ann Benton to Elizabeth McDowell
                Benton (1794–1854) and Thomas Hart Benton (1782–
                1858) at Cherry Grove, Virginia, the McDowell family
                plantation.

April 9, 1840   The wedding of Russian diplomat Count Bodisco and
                Harriet Williams, Jessie Benton's schoolmate at Miss
                English's Female Seminary in Georgetown. Fifteen-
                year-old Jessie as bridesmaid was paired with forty-
                eight year-old groomsman Senator James Buchanan.

October 19, 1841   Marriage of Jessie Ann Benton to John Charles Fré-
                   mont in Washington DC.

1842   Frémont's First Expedition, a US government sup-
                ported trip to map the Oregon Trail as far as the Rocky
                Mountains, formerly known as the Stony Mountains.
                Frémont met and hired experienced guide Kit Carson

at the start of the expedition. Shortly after his return to Washington, Jessie gave birth to their first child, Elizabeth (Lily).

1843	Given the generally acclaimed success of the First Expedition, Congress voted to support a second Frémont-led expedition, this time to map the second half of the Oregon Trail, from the South Pass to Oregon. Frémont's new map guided Americans emigrating to the Oregon country.
1845-1847	Frémont's Third Expedition, and the last one to be government-supported. This expedition put Frémont in California at the time of the US war with Mexico. He was instrumental in securing California for the US. Appointed military governor of the California territory by Commodore Robert Stockton, Frémont refused at first to hand over his authority to US Army Brigadier General Stephen Watts Kearny. Frémont was court-martialed and found guilty for what he claimed was merely his confusion about who had final authority in California.
1847	Jessie and Elizabeth Blair Lee began to write the first of over 80 letters to each other.
July 24, 1848	Birth of Benton Frémont, Jessie and John's second child and first son. The baby died October 6, 1848.
1848–49	Frémont's Fourth Expedition, privately financed, was to explore the Great Basin and to assess territory between the 38th and 39th parallels, (the latitude of St. Louis) for its suitability as a railroad route. It ended unsuccessfully with a loss of $10,000 and ten lives. Jessie got news of these difficulties while she was convalescing in Panama and waiting for a ship to take her to California where she was to meet John.

1850	Frémont elected to the US Senate from California. He was defeated for re-election in 1851 in part because of his anti-slavery views.
May 19, 1851	Birth of John Charles Frémont, Jr. in San Francisco, California.
February 1, 1853	Birth of Anne Beverly Frémont in Paris, France. The baby died July 11, 1853 at the Silver Spring home of Francis Preston Blair, Sr., whose daughter was Jessie's friend, Elizabeth (Lizzie) Blair Lee.
1853–54	The Fifth Expedition, also privately financed for the purpose of exploring a railroad route along the 38th parallel, was deliberately conducted during the winter as a test of the suitability of a central route for the transcontinental railroad. A central route would make the expansion of slavery more difficult than would a southern one, a point important to the Frémonts and the Bentons.
1854	The Nebraska-Kansas Act voided the anti-slavery provision of the Northwest Ordinance and allowed instead for eligible voters in the territory seeking statehood to decide if the new state would be a free or a slave state, a provision proponents called "popular sovereignty," a term opponents found hypocritical.
1854	US Supreme Court decided in favor of the Frémonts' disputed title to extensive land holdings in Bear Valley, Mariposa, California.
1855	The C Street home of Jessie's childhood was destroyed by fire.
May 17, 1855	Birth of Francis Preston Frémont, fifth and last of Jessie and John's children in Washington DC.

1856	Senator Charles Sumner's congressional speech denouncing the Nebraska-Kansas Act and "popular sovereignty" as a swindle.
1856	John Charles Frémont nominated as the first Republican candidate for president.
March 6, 1857	US Supreme Court decided against Dred Scot in a decision that goes beyond the issues in the case to declare that African Americans could not be citizens of the United States. Chief Justice Roger Taney wrote and read the majority opinion.
August 9, 1857	Birth of Francis Preston Blair Lee, only child of Jessie's friend Elizabeth Blair Lee and Samuel Phillips Lee
1861	Frémont appointed major general and given charge of the Western Department in the Civil War, a position he held for only three months.
1863	Jessie published her first book, *The Story of the Guard*, a compilation of documents casting a favorable light on her husband's brief command of the Western Department.
1864	The Frémonts purchased an estate they called Pocaho, near Tarrytown, New York, and retired from political life. Frémont pursued railroad investments.
1873	Frémont declared bankruptcy after the collapse of his scandal-ridden Memphis and El Paso Railroad.
1875	The Frémonts were forced to auction their belongings and sell Pocaho.
1875	Jessie Benton Frémont agreed to write a series of articles on "Distinguished Persons I Have Known" for the *New York Ledger*, and thus brought in much needed income for her family.

1878	Frémont appointed Governor of the Arizona Territory by President Rutherford B. Hayes.
1883	After a 20 year break in their friendship, Elizabeth Blair Lee visited an impoverished Jessie in New York City.
July 13, 1890	Frémont died in New York City.
December 27, 1902	Jessie Benton Frémont died in Los Angeles, California.

Made in the USA
Columbia, SC
27 March 2019